P9-CDW-589

LITTLE OBIE
AND THE FLOOD

*Little Obie had to ride a long, long way from
nowhere, right back to Cold Creek.*

LITTLE OBIE AND THE FLOOD

MARTIN WADDELL

Illustrated by

ELSIE LENNOX

CANDLEWICK PRESS
CAMBRIDGE, MASSACHUSETTS

Text copyright © 1991 by Martin Waddell
Illustrations copyright © 1991 by Elsie Lennox

All rights reserved.

First U.S. edition 1992
First published in Great Britain in 1991 by
Walker Books Ltd., London.

Library of Congress Cataloging-in-Publication Data

Waddell, Martin, Little Obie and the flood / by Martin Waddell ;
illustrated by Elsie Lennox.

Summary: Through hardships and good times,
Little Obie, Grandad, Effie, and newly adopted Marty
grow to become a real family.
[1. Frontier and pioneer life—Fiction.   2. Family life—Fiction.]
I. Lennox, Elsie, ill. II. Title.
P27.W1137Lo 1992 [Fic]—dc20 91-58741
ISBN 1-56402-106-8

10 9 8 7 6 5 4 3 2 1
Printed in the U.S.A.

Candlewick Press
2067 Massachusetts Avenue
Cambridge, Massachusetts 02140

CONTENTS

*Grandad took Obie down
to Bailey's Ford on the wagon.*

Little Obie and the Flood

Little Obie lived with his grandad Obadiah, and his grandma Effie, in their cabin at Cold Creek on the Rock River. It was lonely up there, but they liked it.

One day Grandad hitched up the wagon and took Obie down to Bailey's Ford, at the end of Big Valley. They stopped three miles down the road to pick up Wally Stinson, their next-door neighbor. He came with them on the wagon.

Bailey's Ford was the biggest place around. There were eight cabins there, and Hannigan's Store. Grandad drove to the store and they picked up the provisions. Little Obie and Wally Stinson helped Grandad load the wagon.

"Looks like bad weather's coming," said Mr. Hannigan.

"Yep," said Grandad.

"Rain on the ridge," said Wally Stinson. "I never saw the mountains that black before."

"We'd best be getting back," said Grandad.

That was all he said, but it was enough to make Little Obie think a little. Grandad never said a lot. That wasn't his way, nor Effie's either, but when he did say something, he meant it. It wasn't just talk.

It began to rain on the way back to Stinson's. Wally Stinson and Little Obie got under the canvas, but Grandad got wet driving up front. The wind and the rain lashed at the canvas, and it was very cold. It was dark when they got to Stinson's cabin.

"Stay awhile," said Mrs. Stinson.

"Better get back to Effie," Grandad said. "River'll be rising in the creek."

This time, Little Obie knew Grandad was really worried. He lay in the back of the wagon as it lurched through the rain, and he listened to the roar.

The roar was coming from Cold Creek. The water was rushing and rising. It gurgled around the wagon wheels as they forded the creek, and every minute it rose higher and higher as the rain poured down.

"Never saw the creek so high before, Effie," said Grandad when they were back in the cabin.

"That's so," said Effie.

"I reckon you should set a few things out just in case we need to be moving," said Grandad.

"Maybe so," said Effie.

"I'm afraid," said Little Obie.

"Now see what you've done with your talk!" Effie said to Grandad. She hugged Obie close. Effie was thin, but her body was strong as whipcord. She wanted to give Little Obie some of her strength in case he'd need it, and that was why she hugged him.

Little Obie went to bed, but he didn't get any sleep because of the rain drumming on the roof, the water roaring in the creek, and the noise of Grandad and Grandma shifting things below.

"You asleep, Little Obie?" Grandad said.

"No!" said Little Obie, sitting up in bed.

"We'd best be moving," said Grandad.

"Where are we going?" asked Little Obie.

"To the high ground," said Grandad.

They didn't want to be drowned in the rising water, so they had to move fast. They went in the wagon with all the things that

They didn't want to be drowned in the rising water, so they had to move fast.

The creek had disappeared,
and so had their cabin.

would fit piled up on it. Effie drove the wagon and Grandad drove the animals. Little Obie stayed under the canvas, cold and wet and scared out of his skin.

They made it up as far as the high ground beyond the creek, and there they slept, huddled together in the wagon for warmth and comfort.

When Little Obie woke the next morning, there was water everywhere, right down Big Valley. The creek had disappeared, and so had their cabin. It just wasn't there any more.

"Oh!" said Little Obie.

"Don't be afraid, Little Obie," said Grandad. "The water has risen and the river has burst its banks, but the water will go down again."

"Where's our cabin?" said Little Obie.

"Reckon it just washed away!" said Effie.

"What about the Stinsons?" said Little Obie.

"They should be all right," said Grandad. "It's the folks down the bottom of the valley will get the worst of it."

That started Little Obie thinking.

"What about Marty Hansen and her Pa?" he said. "And Mr. Hedger, and Old Gerd Weber?"

Effie looked at Grandad, and Grandad didn't say a word. He just shook his head very slowly.

"Reckon they'll have gotten their feet wet," said Effie, but like always it wasn't what she said that Obie listened to, it was how she said it. Her eyes were glistening with tears. But then she wiped her nose, and that dried her up. She was old stiff-backed Effie again.

"We ought to go and see what happened to them," Little Obie said anxiously. Marty

Hansen was his friend, and he was worried about her.

"Nobody is going anywhere till the water goes down," said Grandad. "Specially not down the valley. There's no way we'd get the wagon through."

"Maybe Marty got drowned," said Little Obie.

Grandad and Effie didn't say a thing. There wasn't anything they could say.

It rained all day and the next night too, and then the rain stopped. But the water didn't go away. It kept coming off the mountain and rushing down the valley, and the trees and all went with it.

Then the water level started to go down.

It went down all the next day, and the next, and then Grandad said they could try moving down the valley and see how far they could get.

15

There wasn't much left on the low ground but mud and broken trees. They had to lighten the wagon, and even then it sank in deep, and they had to move the mud to get it out again, but in the end they made it down to where Bailey's Ford used to be.

Bailey's Ford nearly wasn't there. Most of it had been swept away. But people had come to Bailey's Ford because there was no other place to go.

Old Gerd Weber and the Stinsons and Mr. Hedger were there, and the Currans and Mr. Hannigan, and some of the other folk from the low ground came straggling in, but Marty Hansen and her Pa didn't come.

"Where's Marty?" Little Obie asked.

"Nobody has seen the Hansens," Wally Stinson said. "There's no getting down to their part of the valley yet."

"I want to go and find Marty, Grandad,"

Bailey's Ford nearly wasn't there.
Most of it had been swept away.

Little Obie said.

"We'll go and look for Marty as soon as we can, Obie," said Grandad. "But there's things that have to be done here first."

They did the things. Little Obie kept thinking about Marty, but he had to be busy too, clearing away the mud and trying to build things up again. There just wasn't any crying time to spare.

"Maybe . . . maybe Marty and her Pa went somewhere else?" Little Obie said to Grandad when they were fixing the stall for Curran's hogs.

"Maybe," said Grandad.

"And maybe not," said Effie, hammering away at her stake. It was a cruel thing to say, but Effie didn't mean it that way. She thought Marty was dead, and that Little Obie would have to face up to it and get on with living with the folks who were left.

"Wally Stinson and me will go down the valley in the morning, Little Obie," Grandad said that night.

"I want to go too," said Little Obie.

"You're staying put," said Effie. "It's no business for a child."

Little Obie wasn't staying put.

Little Obie wasn't made that way.

The next morning when Grandad and Wally Stinson went in the wagon, Little Obie went too. Nobody knew he was going, because he went in the back of the wagon under the straw.

Effie would have skinned him if she'd known.

There was still a lot of water swirling around the dip in the land down by the rock ridge, where Hansen's place used to be.

There was no cabin.

There was nothing much, just mud and

broken trees, trapped against the ridge where the water had left them.

"That's the end of the Hansens," Grandad said to Wally. "Little Obie will be real upset."

"Old Hansen and that girl Marty," said Wally Stinson. "Reckon they never knew what hit them."

Little Obie lay there in the straw, with his feelings all huddled up inside, thinking about Marty and her Pa in the water.

And then . . .

"Look there!" Little Obie heard Wally Stinson say.

The next minute Wally and Grandad were off the wagon down in the mud, heading for the rocks. Little Obie was off after them, only when he jumped off the wagon he fell down in the mud and it was over him, face and all. He dragged himself up and tried

Little Obie lay there in the straw,
with his feelings all huddled up inside.

to run like a little mudball on legs, and there was Grandad holding something limp in his arms, dirt-caked and bloody.

"Marty!" Little Obie said.

"Looks like we got here too late," Wally Stinson said.

But Grandad didn't pay any heed. He was holding Marty close and talking to her, trying to make her alive.

Then Marty opened her eyes and looked at Grandad and Obie. She looked as if she could see them, but she didn't show any sign that she knew who they were, or where she was, or what was happening.

She was like that all the way back in the wagon. Wally Stinson made Little Obie stay up front, and Grandad sat in the straw, hugging Marty to keep what life she had left in her after eight days in the wet and cold.

Little Obie wanted to help Marty, but he

didn't know what to do, and in the end he just sat tight, close up to Wally at the front. Wally said Marty's Pa was dead and they'd all have to be good to Marty because she would hurt a lot, and maybe they were too late and she would die too, but they'd have to pray that she didn't.

When they got back to Bailey's Ford, Effie and Mrs. Stinson took Marty away to Mr. Hannigan's bed by the stove, in the room behind the store.

Marty just lay there and people took turns watching her, even Little Obie.

"Grandma?" said Little Obie one day. "Marty's Pa's dead."

"Reckon so," said Effie.

"What's going to happen to Marty?" asked Little Obie.

"She'd best come with us," said Effie. "If she gets better."

This time they built up the cabin up on the high ground, overlooking the creek.

"I reckon she will," said Little Obie.

And Little Obie was right.

That's how Marty came to Cold Creek to live with Little Obie.

Effie and Grandad and Marty and Little Obie rebuilt the cabin, only this time they built it up on the high ground, overlooking the creek.

"In case the water comes again," Grandad told Little Obie. "Next time we don't want to get our feet wet!"

*"That girl can't read nor write!" Grandad said.
"I don't know what her Pa was thinking of."*

Little Obie and the Owl Pool

New things take some getting used to, and so do new people.

Marty wasn't exactly new people at Cold Creek, but as far as Grandad and Effie were concerned, she still wasn't someone who had been there before. They didn't know her as well as Little Obie did.

"That girl can't read nor write!" Grandad said. "I don't know what her Pa was thinking of."

"You can't neither," Effie said.

"I can," Grandad said. "I can write my name."

"Is that so?" said Effie.

And later Grandad said, "That Marty

don't eat proper! She picks at her food like a chicken. I guess she needs feeding up."

"Food don't grow on trees!" Effie said.

"Some does!" said Grandad.

"And some don't!" said Effie.

And another time Grandad said, "Marty's moping down by the creek again. Some days she don't do nothing but mope. I guess she's missing her Pa."

"Moping never brought anybody back," said Effie.

The way Grandad and Effie said things about Marty sounded hard, but really they were soft inside. They never said a word that would hurt her, because they knew how much she was hurting already.

Little Obie knew it too, but sometimes he couldn't really understand it.

Marty didn't seem like she used to be anymore.

"Hey, Marty!" Little Obie said. "Let's go swimming in the Owl Pool."

"Don't want to go swimming," Marty said.

"Why not?" asked Little Obie.

Marty didn't say why not. She just went and sat on her own on the old tree trunk by the creek, watching the water.

Little Obie had to go swimming all by himself at the Owl Pool, and he didn't want to do that because he wanted to do things with Marty.

"Marty's no use," Little Obie complained to Effie. "She won't go swimming, nor nothing."

"Reckon she's had one swim too many," said Effie. "It's no wonder she won't go swimming after what happened to her Pa."

"Oh," said Little Obie.

"You be good to her, Little Obie," said Effie. "She'll get over it."

But Marty didn't.

She just sat by the creek gazing at the swirling water, and most times she didn't even seem to hear when Little Obie suggested they should go up to the ridge, or how about a tree climb.

One time Little Obie came by the creek and Marty told him to go away, and then she started crying, and the next thing she ran off in the woods. Grandad was cross. Marty didn't come back till almost dusk, and when she did she just went and sat by the fire and never said a thing, but her eyes were all buggy like she'd been crying.

"Is that your doing, Little Obie?" asked Effie, when Marty had gone to bed.

"I didn't do nothing!" Little Obie said. "I don't *have* to do nothing to set her off. She's not like she used to be."

"Marty's been sick," said Grandad.

Marty just sat by the creek
gazing at the swirling water.

*Then the hog bit Effie. It was a
bad bite, right in her leg.*

"She ain't sick now," said Little Obie.

"Just sad," said Grandad. "That's the way it is, Little Obie. And you and me and Effie just got to bear with it till some of the sadness wears away."

"Well, I'm fed up with Marty anyway!" said Little Obie.

For a while he didn't talk much to Marty, in case she'd start crying or run off and he'd get into trouble. But then he started talking again, because inside he was very fond of Marty and he wanted her to be like she was before the flood and not like she was after her Pa was drowned.

Then the hog bit Effie.

It was a bad bite, right in her leg, and Effie had to take to her bed. She couldn't help Grandad no more.

Grandad was worried. He got out the

33

wagon and he went to the Stinsons. He brought back Mrs. Stinson. She did what she could putting Effie to rights, but then she had to go see to her own place and Effie still wasn't right.

Effie got up out of her bed next morning, but she couldn't move much. She just sat in her chair.

"I guess we'll manage," Grandad said, but he wasn't much good at managing. He hadn't the time for it. He needed to be out in the open, looking after things.

Grandad and Little Obie were cutting down trees for a new barn, to make up for the old one that got washed away. Grandad axed the wood and Little Obie stripped the branches off, and together they hauled it to where the new barn was going to be.

When they got back to the cabin at noon, everything was going.

There was a good fire lit, and coffee brewing, and Effie sitting there in the chair with her old bitten leg and a smile on her face, which was something strange because Effie didn't smile a lot. "Reckon somebody just wakened up!" she told Grandad.

There was bacon, cornbread, and squash for their meal, and more coffee, and when that was done and they were all sitting around, Marty was still on the move.

Marty looked after the house at Cold Creek like it had never been looked after before. She looked after Effie too, and kept on doing it until Effie was better and able to move around. Then Marty started doing the wood with Little Obie and helping Grandad with the hogs and the fencing. And when she ate she didn't pick at her food like a chicken anymore; she gobbled it up like a turkey.

"Where'd you learn your manners, girl?"

Grandad said, straight to her face.

"You keep eating, Marty!" Effie said. "Never mind about the manners."

But when Little Obie and Grandad were down by the creek, Effie showed Marty the way people usually eat, without gobbling, and Marty didn't mind one bit.

Effie got hold of Little Obie the next morning and sat him down with Marty at the table. Together they started teaching Marty to read and write. Marty wrote her own name: MARTY HANSEN. It was a little squiggly, but she showed it to Grandad when he came in and he knew what it said.

"You write yours," she said to Grandad.

"Reckon I'll do it for you some other time," said Grandad, and he went off.

"I'm going to be a lady, reading and writing!" Marty said proudly. "Then I'll be real grown-up."

*Together Effie and Little Obie started
teaching Marty to read and write.*

"Don't you be in no hurry to grow up," said Effie. " 'Cause you'll grow up just the same!"

The next time Little Obie went off to the Owl Pool for his swim, Marty went with him.

The Owl Pool was great for swimming because of the deep dark part, and Little Obie didn't think Marty would go in it but she did. She never stopped to think about it. She just dove in.

She still went out by the creek sometimes and sat on the log looking at the water, but now Little Obie sat with her. Sometimes they sat and looked and didn't say nothing, and sometimes they chucked sticks, and sometimes they talked.

Marty didn't forget about her Pa. She couldn't do that, but she didn't spend all day moping anymore either. She wasn't the same Marty as before, but she was getting better and beginning to be happy.

"Reckon it's wearing off now," Little Obie told Effie.

"Reckon so," said Effie.

"Only she still misses her Pa," said Little Obie.

"There ain't nothing we can do about that, Little Obie," said Effie.

Little Obie went off to the creek all by himself, and he sat on the log and looked at the water just like Marty did sometimes. He thought and thought about how he could help Marty, but he couldn't think of anything to do except just being there to talk to her when she wanted him.

So that's what he did.

*Old Gerd was building a cabin all on
his own, a long way from nowhere.*

Little Obie and the Tree

It was fall, and Old Gerd Weber needed help
at Bear Rock, but there was no one to help
him.

He was building a cabin all on his own,
a long way from nowhere. Old Gerd didn't
mind being a long way from nowhere,
because he was strong as a horse and minded
like one. What he was going to do he did,
once he had decided to do it. Grandad
thought Old Gerd should have some help just
the same, because Old Gerd was old and not
so strong as he used to be, although he would
never admit it even to himself.

"I'll go, Grandad," said Little Obie.

"Obie and me!" said Marty quickly. "We'll

both go." Marty wasn't going to be left out
of anything.

"Wait till you've growed a little," Effie said.

"We're fine hands now!" said Little Obie.

"Effie?" said Grandad.

"*Please*," said Marty, and the way she
looked, Grandad could see she was just about
bursting to go.

"Ain't no other help around," Grandad
said. "I can't leave the stock and I don't

reckon they'll come to no harm."

"Maybe so," said Effie. She hemmed and hawed, but in the end they talked her into it.

"You mind what you do now, Little Obie," Effie said. "And none of your tricks, Marty!"

Grandad and Little Obie and Marty got out the wagon and off they went, a long way from nowhere.

Going up to Bear Rock, they could hear

the thunder of Old Gerd's ax chopping at the wood long before they saw him. The crack of it was echoing around the mountain.

"Brought you some help," Grandad said when they came up on Gerd.

"Them children?" said Old Gerd.

"Best I can do!" said Grandad.

"We're the best help there is," said Obie.

"And there ain't no one else," said Marty.

"I can't be looking after 'em," said Old Gerd, doubtfully.

"Reckon they're big enough to look after themselves," said Grandad, and he told Obie never to mind how Old Gerd talked; it was just the way he had grown to be through hunting and trapping on his own all his life, just him and the bears.

Grandad paid no mind to Gerd's grumbles, and Little Obie and Marty jumped right in and started working. Grandad helped to get them started, and then off he went. It was a long way from Bear Rock to Cold Creek, and things needed doing back at the cabin, what with Effie still bad with her leg and the hogs and all.

Little Obie and Marty got on fine. When Gerd felled the trees, they stripped the wood and chopped it, and then they helped draw it back to where the cabin was going to be.

Old Gerd didn't say much, but he stopped complaining when he saw they were real help and not just children for him to be bothered about.

"Reckon I'm the Ax King!" boasted Obie.

"Reckon you're too big for your boots!" said Marty.

Then ... C R A S H!

A tree fell on Gerd Weber.

Old Gerd just lay there moaning. He didn't say nothing.

"Gerd's dead!" said Little Obie.

"No, he's not," said Marty, who knew Gerd wasn't dead because of the moans. "We've got to get that tree off his legs."

"How?" said Little Obie.

"It's too big to move," said Marty. "Maybe we can dig under the tree and get him out."

They tried, but that didn't work. The tree pressed down on Gerd and held him trapped.

"He'll die if we leave him here," said Obie. "We've got to think of something else."

"If we stick some logs under the tree, maybe we can roll it off him," Marty said.

They tried, but that didn't work. The branches of the tree got in the way.

"Strip them off?" suggested Little Obie.

"It would take too long," said Marty. "Gerd would be dead."

Old Gerd opened his eyes.

"Gerd?" Marty said. "Gerd?"

"Aaaaaah," moaned Gerd.

"We can't move the tree, Gerd," said Little Obie.

Gerd said something, a word they didn't understand. He said it over and over.

"What sort of talk is that?" said Little Obie, but Marty guessed what it was. She had heard more talking than Little Obie, from living down in the valley with her Pa and listening to the people going through with their wagons on the way to somewhere else.

"We don't talk German, Gerd," she said. "Say it in our talk."

"*Horse*," said Gerd.

"Horse?" said Little Obie.

"Get the horse!" said Marty. "The horse'll pull it off him." And Little Obie ran to get the horse.

Marty got busy with the ropes. She didn't know how to fix them but Gerd showed her

*The big tree shifted. It didn't shift
very far, but it shifted enough.*

how, in between moaning and groaning about his legs and saying things in German.

Marty fixed the horse to the ropes, and the horse pulled and pulled with Obie on it.

Gerd hollered and yelled, because it hurt when the tree moved.

"Pull! Pull!" yelled Little Obie.

The big tree shifted. It didn't shift very far, but it shifted enough on the logs Marty and Little Obie had jammed in beneath it.

The tree was off Gerd, but he couldn't move much. He yelled when they tried to move him.

"We'll have to get help," said Marty.

"Right!" said Little Obie, and he climbed onto Gerd's horse.

"You mind yourself, now," said Marty anxiously.

Off Little Obie went.

Little Obie was used to riding horses, so

that didn't bother him, but now he had to ride a long, long way, a long, long way from nowhere, right back to Cold Creek.

He rode and he rode and he rode.

There were bad parts

and wet parts,

parts where there was no path,

parts where Obie got himself lost,

parts where he found himself again,

and parts Obie didn't rightly like to remember.

Grandad was up on the ridge, rooting. He saw Little Obie splashing through the creek, and he dropped his pick and came running.

"Grandad! Grandad! A tree fell on Gerd Weber and we got him out from under it but he's lying there moaning about his leg and talking in German and we can't get him to move and maybe he'll die!" Little Obie shouted.

"Hitch up the wagon, Little Obie!" said Grandad, and he fetched Effie from the house, hog-bite leg and all.

Effie and Grandad and Little Obie drove back in the wagon.

It was the fastest wagon ride Little Obie had ever had, and the roughest. They bumped and jostled on the road that wasn't a road, and every time the wagon rocked, Effie's leg gave her a jolt. But she never said a word about the hurt. She just sat there saying it was all right, not minding about nothing but getting to Old Gerd.

Marty was in the trees with Gerd Weber, but Gerd wasn't talking anymore. Marty had him wrapped in sacks, and he was pale like he was dead; but he wasn't dead, because he was breathing thickly, as though he had spittle in his throat.

"I put a splint on him," said Marty. "My

Pa showed me how to make one."

"You're a fine girl, Marty," said Grandad.

Then Grandad and Little Obie got some branches and Grandad lashed them together. They all four got Gerd on the stretcher and carried him back to the wagon. If the carrying was too much for Effie's hog-bite leg, she said nothing about it because it just had to be done.

Old Gerd lay in the back of the wagon with his eyes shut and his legs all bloody, and when he breathed his throat rattled.

They went off in the wagon, real slow. Effie stayed in the back doing what she could for Gerd, which wasn't much, and every time the wagon bumped Gerd groaned. He talked a little in German once, but then he didn't talk anymore.

Old Gerd didn't die.

But he didn't get his leg mended either.

They all four got Gerd on the stretcher
and carried him back to the wagon.

He lay and lay in the cabin at Cold Creek for a long time, until he was as better as he was ever going to be, and then Grandad loaded him up in the wagon and took him into Bailey's Ford and they talked to Mr. Hannigan at the store.

There wasn't anything Mr. Hannigan could do about Gerd's leg either, but Gerd could still talk ordinary talk, as well as German to the people who talked German, so Mr. Hannigan fixed him up a bed and a chair in the store and Gerd stayed there. He did bookwork for Mr. Hannigan, so he wasn't useless and it wasn't all bad.

That was the end of the new cabin a long way from nowhere. It stayed where it was, what there was of it built, for Grandad and Effie and Marty and Little Obie had no need of it, and there wasn't anyone else.

Next time Grandad was down at Bailey's

Ford, Old Gerd gave him a stick of candy a-piece for Marty and Little Obie, to thank them for saving his life.

"That's a big thank-you from Gerd," said Grandad, "considering he's got nothing left to call his own."

"I reckon we did well there," said Little Obie.

"Only what had to be done," said Effie.

"You're a dry old stick!" said Grandad.

"Maybe so!" said Effie.

*It turned out just as well that Effie had
Marty around the place to help her.*

Effie's Birthday

The rough ride in the wagon and the caring that Old Gerd Weber needed when he was mending did Effie no good. It turned out just as well that she had Marty around the place to help her.

"I ain't so young as I used to be, Marty," Effie said, "so you must do your part with the fetching and the carrying."

"Sure thing," said Marty, and she did all she could that winter, and more when she got the chance, and more again when she helped Little Obie and Grandad around the place.

"We got four workers now," said Grandad, and he was real pleased.

"It's because we're growing up," said

59

Marty. "Me and Obie are the hired hands."

"Right!" said Grandad.

"Only we don't get no wages!" said Obie.

Grandad didn't look too pleased.

Marty saw how hurt he was.

"We don't need no wages," she said. "We got nothing to spend wages on!"

Grandad went off to the barn.

"You made him mad, Obie!" said Marty.

"Well, I'm *right*," said Little Obie.

"You know Grandad ain't got no money," said Marty. "Anyway, like I said, you don't need no wages."

"Yes I do," said Little Obie.

"What for?" said Marty. "Go on, you tell me what for."

Little Obie couldn't think what for. There was nowhere he could spend wages, even if he'd had them, because there wasn't anyone else to buy things from at Cold Creek.

"Effie and Grandad *give* you everything, Little Obie," said Marty. "You didn't ought to be asking them about wages like that."

"I wasn't *asking*," said Little Obie. "I was just *saying*."

"Well, you keep your saying to yourself," said Marty.

Little Obie didn't speak to Marty for a whole hour he was so mad at her, and he felt madder because he knew she was right.

The next day Grandad hitched up the wagon and went down to Bailey's Ford. He took Little Obie and Marty with him, and a whole load of sweet potatoes and string beans for Mr. Hannigan to sell in his store.

"I helped grow these," Little Obie told Mr. Hannigan.

"You're a smart critter!" Mr. Hannigan said, and he told Gerd Weber to give Little Obie some aniseed balls.

"Reckon that's your wages," said Marty.

Grandad was a long time in the store settling up with Mr. Hannigan, and he was a longer time still with Mr. Hannigan in the old room at the back of the store. Then he called out for Marty to come in.

Marty came in, and Little Obie came with her because he reckoned Marty might be getting something he wasn't and he wanted his share.

"Here's my stitcher, Hannigan!" Grandad said.

"Young Marty!" said Mr. Hannigan. "Reckon she can do the job?"

"Marty?" said Grandad. "Can you stitch this stuff?"

He showed Marty a whole pile of rags. At least they looked like rags; pieces of old cloth, red and yellow and blue and white and pink, and dots and dashes and striped pieces, all pieces of everything.

"Sure thing," said Marty. "Only what for?"

"Make a nice spread for Effie," Grandad said.

"Grandma's got a spread, Grandad," Little Obie said.

"She'd like a new one," said Grandad. "Specially for her birthday."

"Is it Grandma's birthday?" Little Obie asked.

"Soon will be," said Grandad.

"Sure, I can stitch it up," said Marty, looking pleased and feeling all proud inside. "I'll make her the nicest spread you ever saw."

"Only she's not to see you doing it," said Grandad.

"Right!" said Marty.

They went home and Marty smuggled the pieces of rag into the barn when Effie wasn't around. Every time she got the chance, she hid up there and stitched and stitched.

"Isn't that real pretty?" she said to Little Obie, showing him what she had done.

"Yeah!" said Little Obie, because it was. Marty had every stitch as neat as neat, and the spread looked real good to Little Obie. It was every color of the rainbow and a few besides.

"I reckon it will be the nicest spread there ever was!" said Marty.

"Let me do a little!" said Little Obie, and Marty got him a needle and some thread.

Little Obie stitched, but it didn't come out right somehow. The squares of cloth got all puckered up and funny and wouldn't lie flat.

"How do you do it, Marty?" Little Obie asked.

"Well, I thought anyone would know that!" said Marty, and she showed him.

"Isn't that real pretty?" Marty said to Little Obie,
showing him what she had done.

"It's just easy," Marty said.

"Let me try again," said Little Obie, who didn't want to be beat, especially by Marty.

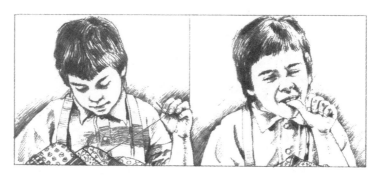

And he tried   and he tried

and he tried.

66

"I reckon you're not cut out for sewing, Little Obie!" Marty said.

"Nobody ever taught me how," said Obie.

"My Pa taught me to sew," said Marty.

And then she didn't say anything for a while because she was thinking about her Pa, and how it used to be before he was drowned in the flood.

"Don't be sad, Marty," Little Obie said. "Let's show Grandad all them colors."

Grandad was real pleased.

"Make a fine present for Effie's birthday," he said.

Little Obie said, "I didn't do none of it," and he stood there feeling bad.

"You stitched some," said Marty, who didn't want Little Obie being upset over a silly thing like not being much of a hand at stitching.

"No, I didn't," said Little Obie. "You took

out all my stitches and did them over."

"You could stitch just one square, very carefully," suggested Marty, trying to be helpful.

"That wouldn't make it right," said Little Obie, and he turned to Grandad. "That's a fine spread, Grandad," he said. "And Grandma will be real pleased. But it was you that thought of it and Marty who made it, and I want Grandma to get something specially from me for her birthday."

"Sure thing," said Grandad, who could see Little Obie was really bothered.

"Only I don't know what to get her."

"That's a real problem, Little Obie," said Grandad.

"Guess you'll have to make her something, like me," said Marty.

"Only I don't know what," said Little Obie gloomily.

"That'll take some thinking about, Little Obie," said Grandad.

"Let's do some thinking now," said Marty.

They sat and they thought, but they didn't come up with anything. Little Obie didn't think he could make pretty things like the spread.

"If I had wages I could buy Grandma something!" he told Marty later, when they were down by the creek.

"Well, you haven't," said Marty. "And it's no use asking, because Grandad's got no money."

"I can't give nobody nothing," said Little Obie gloomily.

"We'll just have to think of something special you can give that don't cost money," said Marty.

"What sort of something?" asked Obie.

"Well, I dunno," said Marty. "But I'm

thinking about it."

"You, me, and Grandad too!" said Obie.

They walked right around the creek thinking, and off up the log thinking, and Little Obie fed the hogs thinking, and ate his food thinking, and went to bed thinking, and then, in the middle of the night when he couldn't sleep because of thinking . . . he *THOUGHT* it!

Only it wasn't a good think.

He *thought* it wasn't a good think, and then he *thought* maybe it was, and then he didn't know whether it was or not, and he went to sleep.

Next day when he was out working on the fence with Grandad, he asked him about it.

"Sounds a fine idea to me, Little Obie!" Grandad said, and right away he led Little Obie to the woodpile behind the barn.

"This piece?" said Grandad.

Grandad led Little Obie to the
woodpile behind the barn.

"Reckon this would do better!" said Obie. He kept on looking till he found what he needed.

"Here's a plank that should do," said Grandad, giving him a short, springy plank from the pile. It was a straight plank from the top of one of Hannigan's barrels.

"I need a stick," said Little Obie.

"Reckon you can cut yourself a stick down by the creek," said Grandad. "Real light straight piece ought to do the job."

Next day Little Obie wasn't around a lot.

Effie thought he was off over the ridge with Grandad, but he wasn't. He was out by the Owl Pool, with the plank and the stick and the old pieces of wood, working with his knife, whittling and gouging and shaping till it was just right.

Next day was the same. Little Obie slipped off to his favorite hidey-hole, the old tree by the Owl Pool, but he wasn't going swimming. He was working. Marty was busy too, finishing off the spread, because the next day coming was Effie's birthday.

If Effie suspected anything, she didn't say a word. But maybe she wondered, because the place was so quiet without anyone around.

The next day Effie got her presents.

"Well, I declare!" said Effie, when she saw the spread.

"That's from Marty and me," said Grandad.

"Not from me," said Little Obie. "I made you something all by myself. I made it 'cause I haven't got no money."

And he gave it to her.

"That's you," said Little Obie, "the one with the big nose. The one with the humpy sort of back is Grandad, and the two little ones, either side, are me and Marty."

"Is that so?" said Effie, fingering her nose and wondering.

"Watch me make them dance!" said Little Obie, who wasn't one bit worried about noses.

And he fitted the stick from the creek in the back of the figures, put the barrel-plank on his knee and put the figures on it, and then . . .

Tap-tap-tap he tapped the plank with his knuckles, and . . . *tap-tap-tap* the four figures danced, all stiff in a row, with their legs jerking up and down. Little Obie had jointed the knees with yarn, and the ankles and the hips, so that all eight wooden legs skipped around just like people dancing.

"That's real nice, Little Obie," Effie said, and she was so pleased she forgot all about having a big nose.

Effie took the plank and put it on her knee

Tap-tap-tap *the four figures danced, all stiff in a row, with their legs jerking up and down.*

and danced the doll family.

Then Grandad did it.

Then Marty did it.

Then Effie did it again.

"Thank you!" she said, and she gave Little Obie a hug, which was something she didn't often do.

"They're us," Little Obie explained again, in case Effie hadn't understood. "That one is me and this one is Marty ..."

"And that's me!" said Effie. "And the big one is Obadiah!"

"Don't look like me," said Grandad, holding his old bones as straight as he could, because no one had ever called him humpy before.

"It's got your wooden head!" said Effie.

When it was late and all the family had gone to bed, Effie heard a noise coming from the big room.

Tap-tap-tap.

She put on her wrap and went to look.

Marty was out of bed, sitting in Grandad's old chair in the firelight, with Effie's new stitched spread around her to keep her warm.

She had the barrel-plank on her knee and she was *tap-tap-tapping* to make the dolls dance.

"Marty?" Effie said, but she said it very softly because she didn't want to frighten her.

Marty never heard her. She was talking to the dolls.

"You're our family," she said. "You're me, and that one's Grandma with her big nose, and that one is Grandad with the humpy back, and the little skinny one down at the end, that's Little Obie."

"A-hem!" said Effie, clearing her throat.

Marty looked up.

"Back to bed, Marty!" Effie said.

Marty went back to bed.

Effie didn't.

She sat down in the firelight in her own chair, with the new spread around her to keep the hog-bite warm. She picked up the barrel-plank, and rested it on her knee. Then she stuck the stick in the back and let the doll family dance and dance.

Tap-tap-tap. Tap-tap-tap.

The Marty doll danced, and the Effie doll danced, and the Obadiah doll danced, and the Little Obie doll danced.

Tap-tap-tap. Tap-tap-tap.

Then Effie stopped tapping the plank and the doll family stopped dancing.

"Time we was all in bed!" Effie told them, and then she looked up, quick-like, to make sure no one had heard her.

No one had, so she laid the dolls on the

table and, gathering her new, all-the-colors-of-the-rainbow spread around her, she went back to bed, a year older but years younger as well.

Effie went to sleep.

Everybody slept.

A whole family, together in their cabin at Cold Creek on the Rock River.